Victor Rochas

Cuba under Spanish Rule

Victor Rochas

Cuba under Spanish Rule

ISBN/EAN: 9783337382247

Printed in Europe, USA, Canada, Australia, Japan

Cover: Foto ©Andreas Hilbeck / pixelio.de

More available books at **www.hansebooks.com**

CUBA

UNDER

SPANISH RULE.

By DR. Vte de ROCHES.

(From the " Revué Contemporaine.")

——:o:——

NEW YORK :

GREAT AMERICAN ENGRAVING AND PRINTING COMPANY,

Nos. 21 & 23 Ann Street.

CUBA UNDER SPANISH RULE.

The Queen of the Antilles it appears is about to free herself from Spain, either by means of an arrangement between the United States and the Spanish Government, or by the insurrection, which, unaided, in the end, will bring about the same result. The separation from the mother country is now a fact inevitable. It would not be uninteresting to examine the causes which have brought about the breaking up of former relations. But this will be easier of comprehension when one looks to the administration of affairs, to the judicial and taxation *regime*. He will then see how legitimate and just are the causes which have impelled the Cubans to raise aloft the standard of revolt. This work was written before the late events which have taken place; its author lived in the Island during many years, and speaks of nothing except what he saw, and although a victim of the system there practiced, he has observed the strictest impartiality. If at any time the recital of sad events has disturbed his equanimity, which always admits of excuse, yet in truth he has copied the very words of official documents whose authenticity is undisputed. The reader has under eye an exact picture of Spanish dominion in Cuba, and can detect from an examination of the same consequences which enable him to judge whether or no the mother country has in good faith fulfilled her duties or compromises, in short, he can determine on which side of the Atlantic are right and justice in these matters to be found.

Above all, the head of the Government is enthroned as a great dignitary, reuniting in himself the civil authority as well as military, and is, moreover, protector of the religious authority; takes as titles Captain General, Governor Superior Civil of the

Isle of Cuba, President of its *Real Audiencia* (highest court), and Vice-Royal Patron of its Churches. And all this is true, for he commands the army and marine, and has the direction of all branches of administration, including that of the treasury; watches over civil justices; regulates and even suspends the tribunals, that extraordinary tribunals may supply their places whenever he may think the event demands it. In respect to religious affairs he has not much sway. Beyond having the church bells rang at his approach into any of the town and villages, he yields to the bishops the right to do what they please; but unless they do or cause this thing to be done, he sends them to Spain, as has happened. Besides, the Captain General is president of all the societies and corporations established in the island. Without his presence, or that of those delegated by him, nothing can be done; not even can a meeting of shareholders of a stock company be legally held. His powers are unlimited, as are also his functions; he gives no account of his conduct other than to the government of the mother country; and then only to the Sovereign, when, as happened with General Lersundi, who was freed from interference on the part of the Minister of the Colonies before accepting the position. The decree of the 25th May, 1825, which regulates his powers, confers upon him " the full use of the faculties which by royal ordinance are conceded to governors of besieged towns." There is no remedy as against him while in office, and when he has given up the command to his successor, complaints are heard in the illusory *juicio de residencia.*

Beyond this, and until this epoch arrives, there exists no remedy to him who complains, other than remaining in patience and advancing large sums for the purpose of carrying on the trial. If he be young, and is disposed to fight it out, and besides has money to back him, perhaps he may succeed in obtaining a sentence which declares that he has been a victim of ill-used power—nothing more. A functionary as much occupied as the Captain-General, should be well remunerated. He is in the receipt of a salary of $50,000 per annum, and has a palace in the city and a chateau in the country.

This charge would be a little too heavy for Spain, where the Prime Minister is paid only $6,000 per annum, but it is the Isand of Cuba that pays the expenses ; yes, this sum it pays unaided to its royal jailor! Besides, if he wishes to raise unlawful taxes, who is to hinder him ? True, all do not do this, but, without doubt, many have so done.

M. D'Harponaille, in his admirable work on the Island of Cuba (La Reina des Antilles, Paris, 1850, says, in speaking of the administration of General O'Donnell, from 1843 to 1848 : The clandestine introduction of African slaves encountered no opposition in him, though 'he received but a small tax or benefit on account of his vice-royal concessions. Such was the case also with the greater part of his predecessors. On arriving he intimated that he was an enemy of the slave trade, but we, at least, know that he was not of that which it produced for the Governor. "For each negro there was paid an ounce, or $17, to this personage. The custom, from long *user*, has acquired the force of a law. Here we should, perhaps, stop, but it would be proper to add, such scandalous contracts were entered into that his wife had the control of the monopoly, that which occasioned such noise."

After the Captain-General came the Commanding-Generals, the Civil Governor of the Departments. These high functionaries are looked up to with nearly the same respect on the part of those governed by them as the Captain-General himself, under whose direction, more or less, they move.

They increase as much as possible the authority, civil and military, preside over the City Council of the capital, and intervene in public works through the lieutenants of the Governor, settle and arrange the contributions, whose sum is fixed by the Sovereign authority, apply at will the correctional punishments by prison and fines, up to forty days in the one case, and $50 in the latter. Taken from the line of the militay, in order that they may not lose the custom of governing they manage a department as a military headquarters, and treat the people as common soldiers. Their pay is $12,000 per annum ; they are given, besides, houses and other accessories.

The governors of the departments have under their orders the lieutenant-governors, commanders of the jurisdictions which are in number 31. These are divided into *partidos* at the head of which there is a functionary named by the governor, and who entirely depended upon him for orders. As to the administration of these lower functionaries nothing more appropriate can be said than what was the opinion of the Cuban delegates to Madrid in 1866: "The lieutenant-governors invested as they are, with the military command and the presidency of the councils, as well as directions of the captains of *partidos* in their small precincts, are the sources of a great calamity for the Island of Cuba. Nominated by the governor superior civil, without the slightest bond of interest with the inhabitants whom they are sent out to govern, without the slightest care for the opinion that may be formed of their conduct in the locality where they go to pass a few years of their lives, and to which they never expect to return when once their commands are given up, they become petty tyrants who cannot bear any sort of contradiction. If disposed to be bad, all the avenues towards becoming rich are open before them, to the cost of the people governed. If influenced by sentiments of honor—they are, at any rate, ignorant of the wants of their districts, and have no personal interest other than in inaugurating some work, however useless it may be, that may perpetuate the remembrance of their administration. This, let it be said, does not prevent the greater part of the municipal resources from being consumed in expenses of representation, house expenses, and pay of employees. We have seen various localities in the interior of the Island where though the municipal moneys levied and collected were large enough yet were almost entirely consumed in pay of employees, house rent and furniture, and if there were any funds remaining unspent these were devoted to the laying out of a *paseo* or square in which some stone was found erected to the honor of the captain-general, his wife, or daughter.

As to the captains of partido, whatever might be said would be insufficient to convey a definite idea of the truth. They come to the different districts with a pay of $50 to $100 a month for self and family, which, however does not hinder them from growing richer day by day. We prefer to be silent on this point, referring as we do to the captain-generals who have governed the island, and whom we have heard often deplore their own impotency in the matter of preventing the frauds upon which the *captains del partido* fattened and grew rich. "*Informaciones de Reformas en Cuba. Tome 2o, p. 136.*"

If, after having examined analytically the mechanism administrative, we should reconstruct it synthetically, we would bind ourselves in the presence of a despotic government of the first class ; looking to the fact that it can condemn to prison, banish from the country, or send out at call and without the intervention of the tribunals whom it chooses, and even go so far as to confiscate property ; seeing that it imposes and distributes the taxes without the tax-payers having a hearing in the premises ; inasmuch as the country has neither a provincial nor a municipal representation, not even for the purpose of looking into its necessities. Nor has it the right to discuss its own proper interests, or to participate with the government in the direction of public affairs. It is not permitted even to publish opinions or thoughts without a severe and fastidious censorship shall have been previously passed ; and to this is sometimes added an examination by the ecclesiastical authority.

The municipal representation exists really only in appearance—it is a mere fantasm. Chosen by the government from a list presented by the largest tax-payers, there is nothing of the independent connected with it, nor is there anything initiative in it. It has no power to control local interests, nor to fix or distribute the municipal taxes, except under the presidency of the Governor and with ratification of the Captain-General. The administration of real property, the use of the taxes, works of public utility, all these in fact are in the hands of the Governor, and the intervention of the Council is for nothing more than to give an aspect of legality to what is done. Thus we behold the principal towns in a condition of filth amounting to repugnance, without communications, with streets seldom paved, and through which run deep sewers that the rain heaps full, and in which all the filth of the neighborhood is deposited. There are no decent hospitals, nor asylums for the mad. There is an establishment in Havana, but in the other towns lunatics and madmen are placed in the common jail, as was the case in the middle ages. These towns are left without means of any kind to prevent the approach of disease, or to succor the indigent; and notwithstanding this, the Councils are perplexed by the weight of an enormous debt that the tax, however great it be, never pays off. Such is the state of the large towns. What succeeds in the smaller ones can be readily imagined. This is so in Santiago de Cuba, the second city of the isle, which for eighteen months has not paid its gas bills, nor police, nor school expenses, and all the other towns are in nearly the same fix. Moreover, there is no regular line of roads which unites the centres of the population together. The administration of the towns is an index of the administration of the whole country. Here we see the fruits of an absolute government imposed upon the country by the Mother Country.

To carry out this *regime* the ministers who succeed each other in Spain, free themselves from their political compromises by sending out to Cuba, upon large pay, functionaries without antecedents which justify their selection. At the head of an irresponsible government there is found a public accountability and another one secret, a scheme of taxes officially promulgated, and another one of a private character. So in fact while there figured in the tax scheme of Spain for the year 1866 the sum of $4,400,000 of Cuban money there is no mention of pensions paid out of these same moneys, neither of the expenses of Fernando Po, which are four times that sum. Neither does it include the unjust exactions occasioned by reason of the cost of the St. Domingo war, or those of the Mexican, Chilean or Peruvian difficulties, nor the $6,000 paid to the Queen's confessor. The Mexican and St. Domingo expeditions sailed out from Cuba and were paid for out of her money. All the coal of the Pacific squadron, was contracted and paid for at Havana. Mendez Nunez (the admiral) came to Sto. de Cuba for provisions. The decree of 19th October, 1868, reveals to us the fact as to Padre

Claret's pension, which it suppressed. But is it less rediculous and unjust to make Cuba pay the expenses of Fernando Po than the pension of P. Claret, by the use of the same powers as were exercised in the other house? It is because the ministry in Spain was changed, and not the relations between Spain and Cuba; there is one ministry more and one Padre .Claret less.

The Treasury Minister has no means of getting out of the difficulty except by putting his hands, unopposed, into the cash box of Cuba and Porto Rico. There was a time, it was two years ago, when the treasury played traitor and showed signs of insolvency, when, in fact, the government having drawn out all the capital of the Spanish bank of Havana, reserved to pay its circulation, was forced to pay its highest interest bearing obligations with depreciated paper, or authorize the Bank to do so in contradiction of its charter and of the law regulating the payment of its notes. Then commerce and industry had to do business without money. In this contingency a forced circulation of the notes was ordered by the government; hence a panic spread through all classes, and numerous bankruptcies were the result, hence the discontent of the country increased, and this ran into insurrection. This government, let us resume, is a political monopoly which excludes popular representation, an intellectual monopyly which keeps in reserve the emission of thoughts, a religious monopoly which imposes only one mode of belief and worship, the monopoly commercial which imposes its flag and its products. All these assertions will be proved in this relation.

II.

This despotic government is very expensive, but has it the merit of preserving order in a heterogenoeus populations. Let us examine this question.

If we look to the order which reigns on the sugar estates we find that it is due to a discipline established, a long time past, by the proper inhabitants of the Island, and on them it reflects honor. Is it less a matter of surprise to see the negroes of a sugar estate obey a few whites than to see the large crew of a ship of war out in the midst of the ocean obey the staff which commands it? The relative leniency of the slavery of our days, the interested solicitude, in part of the master, the prestige that the white exercises over the negro, and that which the free man has over the slave, aid as much as discipline in the matter of maintaining order. The government seldom intervenes between the master and the slave; should the latter fly away the agents of the public force, rare in the country, take no steps towards arresting him. This is the duty of the master, and if unable to do it himself he employs a slave catcher, who, for five dollars, does the work. Ordinarily he does not even do that, but waits for the slave to return voluntarily, which he generally does with a *padrino* (protector), who is some inhabitant of the vicinity. It is very rare that the negro is away more than four or five days without desiring to return to the hut where lives his mother, his wife, or his children, to his little patch, his *corral*, to the companions of his diversions as well as the sharers of his labors, in a word, to the domestic hearth and its accessories. There are some negroes who never return. These build on the highest mountains or in the deepest woods, what in the country are called *palenques*. Them the government permit to remain in tranquillity, notwithstanding the harm they cause to travellers and to estates. The government has so little to do with established order that for two months after the occupation of the Eastern Department by the insurgents servile labor continued as before. The rebels proclaimed emancipation at the beginning of January, and the negroes still did not move; it was found necessary to tear them away from the *ingenios*, and by the middle of February the greater part had gone back to them again. Up to this time no serious violence had been committed on the persons of the whites by the negroes, except in the death of a man, in whose house a slave had been assassinated, but by whom was unknown. Nor down to this time was there any proof that the slaves had any ideas of vengeance against their masters, or that they had been illy-treated

Persons who form an opinion of the social state in Cuba from the history of our ancient colony of St. Domingo find it difficult to comprehend how freemen of color can live in good under-standing under the pressure of a government, strongly contitut-ed, which keeps them in peace ; there are 260,000 against 794,000 whites. These are equal to the latter before the laws in every thing affecting civil rights, and so far as those denomi-nated political are concerned, neither the one or the other enjoy them. There are distinctions founded in old, musty privileges, but repeated intermixing and fortune cause these to disappear. The public voice "besides" anticipates those favored by birth and fortune, and discerns the difference between gentlemen and people whose color and conduct betray their mixed origen. In another generation all this will have disappeared.

It is easy to understand that the government has no difficulty in keeping good order where no one desires to disturb it. But let us ask, Has peace always existed without clouds ? and has the free colored population ever relied upon the slaves to inau-gurate a social war ? or have the negroes ever made an attempt to break their chains ? There has never been a serious project of anything of the kind, though it was supposed in 1844 that a conspiracy had been discovered in Matanzas on the part of blacks.

In every manner this conspiracy was greedily used as a means to make money by the police and military commissions. "That no complot was formed," says a Spanish author who held important trusts on the Island at this period, "cannot be denied, but never to the extend supposed. That in the proceedings di-rected by the military commissions and by a multitude of sub-agents there was, want of legality and impartiality, such as is demanded among civilized people when the matter of life and death to men is to be decided, needs no other proof than the punishment inflicted by the superior authority upon many fiscals (state attorneys) because of their venality and excesses, the suicide of two of these and the flight of others when they saw that their infamy had been discovered. The Secretary Don Pedro Salazer was condemned to prison. Three thousand colored persons were sentenced, the proof against whom was deficient in material points for the execution of projects which were attibuted to them.* "The banished, the condemned to prison were numerous, as were also the executions. The best poet of the Island, Gabriel Valdes, called Placido, was one of the victims," although, "as said Pezeula," his criminality does not appear to be other than a sentence without explicit grounds." His ardent muse inspired him even while surrounded by iron bars. He went up to the place of execution reciting his " Plegaria a Dior," the veritable song of the swan, the best of his poms.

This happened during the government of O'Donnell. Ten years before, General Tacon had instituted military commissions in a time of profound peace. But disorder and corruption were the foundations for the chronic state of the country under the *regime* of that government. It will be seen from the work already cited, that these tribunals fulfilled their mission by proceedings identical to those which gave them birth. M. D'Harponville relates the facts as conforming to a sentence pronounced in Madrid. ("Reine des Antilles," p. 464, first edition.)

In 1868, Captain-General Lersundi betook himself to the same resource, in order to aid—though in ordinary times—the impotency of the courts, "considering," as he said in his decree of 4th of January, 1868, "the crimes, which are as frequent as scandalous, now being committed, we withdraw from the ordinary tribunals the trials of cases of homicide, robbery and incendiarism, whatever may have been the circumstances under which these were perpetrated by the guilty parties, or their accomplices and those who harbor them, without distinction. These shall be tried by military commissions, established at Havana, Santiago de Cuba, Porto Principe, Villa Clara, and Pinar del Rio. The specified charges will be remitted along with the criminal, if he has been arrested, to the disposition of the President of the Commission within twenty-four hours, and the cause shall be put to trial in the quickest time possible, under the personal responsibility of the President of the Judges and Fiscal

---

*Diccorinario de la Ysla de Cuba.   Tomo 4 p. 639.

(attorney of government), who will not forget for an instant that the principal object in the installation of these commissions military is to have a speedy disposition of matters, in order that justice may be as prompt as inexorable," &c.

Notwithstanding the unfavorable antecedents of this institution, and the want of confidence which the intervention of government and military inspires, this hard measure of Lerscudi was well received by the great majority of the best people in the island. It is a sad thing to say so, but the ordinary tribunals, inattentive as corrupted, only commanded the respect of the good. Who did not feel himself menaced as well as his property when he saw crime unpunished and its authors go out of the prison-houses more audacious than ever ? Thus a subsequent proclamation assured the criminals and those who testified against them, " tnat once condemned the former should not again make their appearance in the country," to the end that the latter might not stand in fear of their vengeance. This assurance was opportune, because the vicinage was accustomed to see the criminals escape public vengeance as well as that inflicted by confinement in prison, which enabled them to avenge their informers and prosecutors. Without doubt, the military commissions as well as the civil tribunals might be composed of venal and corrupt judges, but the rapidity with which the proceedings were carried on, far from inspiring, alarm was considered as a guaranty against the uncertainty of legislation, the complication of judicial acts, the abuse of jurisdiction, and the fearful artifices of a shameless forum. I spoke of the uncertainty of legislation ? This results from the multitude of codes which govern us. We have the Law of the Indies. the Nueva Recopilacion, La Novissima, the laws of tne Toro, El Fuejo Juzo, El Fuero Real, the law of Enjuiceamiento Civil, El Bando de Gobernacion y policira, and de Partidas laws, without mentioning the Ecclesiastical code, the Ordonnances of War and Marine and La Jurisprudence est ablecida.

The tribunals are not less numerous. There are Justices of the Peace of the first instance and Alcal des Mayores, both civil and criminal ; Tribunals of Appeal or Real Audiencia, Tribunal of Casacion at Madrid, Juzgado Ecclesiastico, Court of Military Orders, of War, of Treasury, of Marine, Tribunal of Commerce, and, in short, Military Commissions from time to time.

The proceedings are complicated to a certain extent, because of the matter of jurisdiction. *Fuero* signifies more than jurisdiction ; it comprehends, also, the idea of privilege. The clergy, the military, the marine, the grandees of Spain, the members of the military orders of knighthood, those who are decorated with certain honors have their appropriate tribunals, that is to say, there are appropriate tribunals for them.

All those nearly related to—or even holding distant reations with those corporations enjoy, their own proper privilege, such, as for instance, the military and the marines retired, the auxiliaries and supernumeries of the army and marine, the counsellors and *escribanos* (notaries) of the courts, their wives, children and servants. If one of these privileged persons be sued for a debt, and if he be adjudged to pay the sum demanded, he will immediately ask for another place of trial, and it becomes a matter of necessity to commence a new proceeding and pay all the costs accrued.

One of the most remarkable things is that which raises a question of privilege as between the renter of a house and its owner. The first can leave the house whenever it suits him without any notification, but the owner cannot force him to leave the house unless he shall have neglected for three consecutive months to pay the rent, and then a fixed time will be granted him within which to procure another house. If the renter pays faithfully the owner, the latter cannot demand that the house shall be vacated. This he can obtain only by way of compromise ; such as inhabiting it himself, or by shutting it up for four years. In no other way can the possession be obtained or the price raised, notwithstanding the fact that the value of rent of houses in the neighborhood may have risen in value. However hard these conditions may be for the owner, he might get along very well in bearing them, but, unfortunately, he finds himself subjected to other conditions still worse ; for nothing is easier than fer renters of bad faith to buy up the judge to the end that he may give them a long time to pay what is due, and the owner considers himself lucky if at the end of a year he should succeed in getting possession of his house, though losing all the rent. To avoid such prejudices, such scenes as these related below occur in which the sentiments of the renter are appealed to : " My friend, be so good as to leave my house. In such case I demand nothing of you for the last six months." " My dear sir," answered the other, " I am so much in love with your house that it would cause me much pain to leave it." " Be just," replies the owner, " I will pay the cost of moving." " I am always at your service," sneers the renter, but I am well here." '"Very well, we must go to law." " Well, we will go into the courts then," is the last answer.*

In Cuba it is not the creditor who passes along with high head before his debtor, for the latter occupies the sidewalk ; and this is easily understood, for as there is no such thing as imprisonment for debt, the debtor readily runs the risk of prison. son. In 1837, Tacon took out of the Havana prison a mason who had been shut up there for forty years, because he had demanded of a marquis his dues, and who probably pleaded to the jurisdiction of the court. In 1867, at Santiago de Cuba, a tailor asked of a rich man, for the second time, for the amount of his bill, which was a just one. The debtor put him off to the Greek kalends, which excited the indignation of the creditor, and he replied with some warm expressions. In any other country the matter would have gone at once before a competent tribunal, which would most probably have decided against the debtor ; but here, on the contrary, it was brought before the court of a drunken governor, who without delay, gave the decision in favor of the rich man and against the poor one, in favor of the friend and against the man unknown, and ordered the tailor to prison. It would seem that with so many especial jurisdictions, the ordinary tribunals could do all the labor occuring in the year; but this is not so, if we believe the statement of the Regent of the Real Audiencia in his opening discourse

---

* General Dulce slightly modified the rent-law by decree of 16th February, 1869. It was but little bettered.

pronounced 2d of January, 1868, wherein he said : " The number of processes determined in the different courts of the Audiencia for the year 1866, amounted to 8,453, of which 4,673 ended by a sentence of *sobresamiento* (discharged for want of proof.)* This is not because the worthy part of the people are brawlers or disposed to wrangle, but for the reason that the bad have the means of carrying on the litigation gratuitously, which is effected by having themselves previously declared, either really or pretendly insolvent—that which confers another additional privilege or right of jurisdiction.   Though the judges might be incorruptible and infallible, it is readily seen that in a proceeding so complicated, resources minister to the want of probity.   There are, indeed, accommodations in the administration of Cuban justice, and with a few humble exceptions, the judges are not insensible to - bribery.   At each change of the ministry there is a complete change of the *personnel* of those administering justice ; and from their offices at Madrid the larger part of the magistrates for the island come.   Ignorant of the interests of the country on local customs, they cannot form a correct opinion even were they honest and possessing experience and a sense of justice.   In short, the Cubans are deprived of the precious guaranty afforded by trial by jury ; and a single alcalde mayor renders alone, unaided, a decision which disposes of a man's life!   This, however, is subject to the revision and ratification of the Real Audencia. The influence produced by the decision of the judge, who first tried the prisoner, can be readily divined.

This system of justice has been passed upon by one of the best known Spanish Magistrates, Varques Quivpo, fiscal that was of the Real Audicencia at Havana.   " If justice was not dearer," says he, this would be only the half of the evil.   Is it not worse

---

* The document shows the crimes and misdemeanors to have been as follows : 4,000 offences against public order—that is to say, 35 more than in the previous year. 2,033 attempts against the person—348 more than previous year. 2 867 against property— 202 more than the year before ; 52 charges for deceit—12 more than in previous year ; 51 against employees while in the exercise of their functions—7 more than previous year. The crimes were : a patricide, three infanticides, 160 homocides (13 more than he year before). Here is an example of the progress of moral and public order!

when dearly-bought justice purchased is not then obtained, notwithstanding the painful sacrifice made?*

In France, in England, in Spain it is certainly not cheap, but one can expect reasonably to obtain it. This is not the case in the Island. It is not so in the Island, we repeat 'it. Reform does not consist in diminishing the expenses of justice which would be indeed, desirable, but in the fact it may be secured. Nor can this be done, unless there be adopted a press law, clear and explicit, which will make effective the judicial responsibility, While these desired reforms are delayed, the prosperity of the Island is retarded by the nullity of legal guaranty, by a want of reciprocal confidence in business affairs, by a timidity of capital and its consequent scarcity, because the lender knows that he must take into account the danger of loss, and so varies the rate of interest. Thus it is discovered that the great obstacle to the progress of a country is not the insalubrity of the soil, nor the heat of the climate, the insufficiency of the roads, snd their little security, but consists in the want of legal guarantees which every man sesks for his liberty, his life and property.

It is clear that the absence of legal guarantees conduces to the taking of arbitrary means of order and security in order to supply them, whence springs the continual intervention of the authorities in the domain of the tribunal, and the shipping away *en masse* of the people, which policy Tacon, O'Donnell, and Lersemdi thought themselves obliged to recur to.

Without desiring to go back further than O'Donnell's time, let it be said, that he, desiring to purge the Island of vagabonds adopted the idea of colonizing a desert isle, to favor the establishment of an industrial association, and to enrich, at the same time, his pocket. " A company," says M. de Harponville, " was formed to exploit the Isle of Pines, which is situated to the south of Cuba."†

This company was not slow in making money, but it owed this to the immoral and efficacious protection which the Captain General lent to it.

---

*Informe fiscal of Dr. V. Vazquez Quipo. Madrid, 1845.
† La Reine des Antilles, pp. 124.

The slave trade which he protected, or, at any rate, tolerated, inspired him with the idea of making white slaves, and, protected by the omnipotence and want of responsibility of his government, he did not fear to order to forced labor in the mines free white men. This order fell upon the people of the towns, and,' above all, in the country, without questions being asked, or condemnations having been made. The pretext was that these men were vagabonds and of bad habits. The company made a present to his Excellency and to his wife of 200 shares, and while the Governor-General was enriching himself the sycophants, who held the *carte blanche* to gather up men, made certain pretended vagabonds pay very dearly for their exemptions, some of whom were compelled to pay for their release as much as their weight in gold!

General Lersemdi had recourse to the same heroic remedy, but he did not make any capital by it. He contented himself with taking from the Havana prisons those who had fallen, for the second time in crime, the incorrigibles, and those who were upon process for correction by the police, and whose causes had not been ended by the laborious Audiencia, and these were embarked for Fernando Po on the coast of Africa. As a means of security and of warning to those interested he caused a list to be made up of all those on the Island who lived without occupation of any kind, and who could not show some means of subsistence.

If arbitrary methods had not always produced bad effects, we should not complain though the sword might be hurtful and of two edges. What a suitable pretex, so convenient to get rid of all independent characters who, exhibited any spirit toward the government? Proceedings so expiditious might be deemed unjustifiable, even if supposed to be applied by perfect beings. But if the captain-general were so, does that follow that his subalterns are so too? With the exception of a few old officers who are found in the body of police, it is a thing well-known that the men, who do the seizing are the dregs of the population. This the frequent discharges from employment for prevarication and numerous examples, which might be cited, abundantly prove.*

Justice only condemns to be sold those slaves sentenced whose masters are unwilling to pay the costs of the cause, doubtless, to the end that they may commit if they feel disposed, other crimes !

The governor has an established gambling house. This beavrs the pompous title of " Royal Lottery of the Ever Faithful Island of Cuba," which up to 1822, had already made for its owner, the (king), $5,865,625. Pezuela in his Dictionary calls the lottery, the branch of service especially working in the interests of the Treasury, with more certainty than any other for the sources of revenues." The Administration receives to itself as a product the one-fourth part of the capital to which the sum of the tickets amount. In 1864, 546,000 tickets were sold at the rate of $16 each, which made up the enormous amount of $8,736,000. When the taxes had been increased at the time of the crisis, the passion of all classes, including the slaves, was converted into a perfect furor. For this reason, the government drew, in addition to the eighteen ordinary lotteries, two other extraordinary, and of high-priced tickets, all without prejudice to the lottery at Madrid, whose billetes were also distributed throughout the island. The government does not admit competitors. Nothing is more immoral than this official institution, which extracts all the gains of the poor, and diverts him from labor and honest earnings with the deceptive hope of a fortune acquired at a single stroke! The desire of gaming is fostered by this means, and it becomes general; for, notwithstanding the

---

*F. Dargo, Captain of partido of Jarrigua, says "El Oriental," of Hognin has run away with the tax-money, (July, 1868). " In the night of June 1, 1887, says El Boletin de Cardenas, some Chinamen led before the local authorities a white man tied, who had a knife (punal), saying that this man and a companion who made his escape " tried to rob them. The prisoner was no other than a night-watch, and his companion had been discharged 15 days before because of his bad conduct." Do the police add themselves to the number of thieves ? This would indicate a propensity for monopoly.

† When a slave is apprehended for a great misdemeanor he is given over to justice because of the fear of expenses in defending him, which may be more than his value Whether guilty or no the expense must be paid, if absolved, immediately ; if condemned, after his punishment has been expiated.

legal prohibition of private lotteries, and of gaming, each one has his own lottery under the special title of raffle." Men raffle off their horses or watches—the ladies their bracelets and dresses.

Gaming penetrated formerly into the convents,* and in a nearer epoch (1858 to 1862), extended its green table as far as the public square of Santiago de Cuba on the feast days, paying for the privilege a tax to the City Council, which was for the benefit of works of public improvement. Gambling goes on in concealed places where people of importance do not feel ashamed to go. In the country the *veguero* bets away his crop of tobacco while growing, and the overseer of a farm gambles off at times his oxen, hard pressed as he may be to support his family. The police cannot prevent it. More disposed to annoy than to be vigilant in the cities, there is hardly any in the country, where each *capitain del partido* counts three or four guards on horseback, and whose principal business is to carry about the mails. The form stifles the essence, the letter kills the spirit that which is strictly insisted upon ; nothing beyond is deemed necessary.

To save appearances—this is the essential, and to spend much for stamped paper, which is for the interests of the state. In a country which is one-fourth part as large in extent as Spain, and whose inhabitants do not number beyond 1,400,000 inhabitants, which is equivalent to 289 for each square league, the same police regulations are applied as in Spain. Not not only the rural police and judicial proceedings are regulated in this manner, but all the branches of administration likewise. "The proof of the want of order in the government which we deplore is the immense number of rules and dispositions derogatory, in great part, the one of the other, in all matters of administration, and which no one, even those who are to administer them, knows. These dispositions, made by persons who are are constantly being relieved from duty, and who consequently cannot become familiar with the country that they go out to aid in ruling, cannot produce other effect than to place the government in ridicule. As for example, the famous rural ordinances of

---

* Statement of Gen. Tacon on the state of the country after his arrival.

1856, (afterwards amended), by which premiums were conceded for capturing wolves, foxes and other ferocious animals, when there were never such animals to be found in the country, but whose stuffed skins were occasionally to be met with in cabinets of natural history." *(Informacion Sobre Reformas, New York,* 1867.)

A Spanish writer, Alcala Galiano, in his book entitled, "Cuba in 1858," says, while criticising the mania for rules : " No one knows with exactitude that which has been ordered, nor that which has been put forth as an order, nor when nor how the order should be applied." All of us who have lived in Cuba are fully advised in this particular. Go into an office of the government upon any matters of business. " My friend, where is your petition ?" is the first question asked. " But I come only to ask about a very simple thing. I only want a word with you." The reply is : " Put in your written application." On the following day the party comes in with a memorial on stamped paper, as a matter of course. " Well, come in day after to-morrow." That day arrives, but the business is not arraigned, and the further answer is given, " Come to-morrow morning." At last the matter is favorably passed upon, but nothing has been really done. Should my adversary practice a little underhand managment, I am stopped. Certain gifts (moneys) serve as an additional compensation to subalterns badly paid, who serve as intermediaries between the petitioner and the Superior Authority. This is a compensation which makes up for the delays of payment of salaries, which at times are in retard a whole year, andsubject in critical times, (which frequently happen), to be paid with deductions. In truth, the state makes as much out of stamped paper as the employees out of their clients,

IV.

Let us now examine how the other branches of the State are directed, as public works ; public instruction ; worship, for this, unfortunately, belongs to the public service.

Public works figure in the money statement for the fiscal year of 1866–1867, to the amount of $194,591, and the pay of the engineers charged with carrying them on foot up $106,249. Is the proportion strong enough? It seems to me a labor well paid for. And then there are no roads in the country, except those constructed and kept up by the inhabitants. There is not a single port opened or prepared by the hand of man, not a river canalized, not a marsh drained. The bridges over the streams are such as they may be classed, neither good nor bad, and are so useless in time of great rains as that the mails are detained for days, because there is no way of crossing them. There are not 150 miles of roads for wagons in a country whose superfice measures 3,604 square maritime leagues, and which pays 175,-000,000 fcs. ($35,000,000) of taxes. So transportation is carried on by mules, except in the Eastern Department, where there is a sufficiency of railways to answer the purposes of agriculture. But these railways are due only to the public spirit of the inhabitants and to private industry. There is a territory of 111 square leagues, composed of the most beautiful country ever seen, and peopled by 33,673 inhabitants, which vegetates in misery by reason of a want of communications to pass out its products to market; this is the Department of Bayamo.

This section is watered by a majestic river, sixty leagues in length, and whose bottom is deep enough to permit the passage of the largest ship for twenty-two leagues distance. The Spanish caravels of the first century following the conquest went up this stream to take on board wood, suitable for cabinet makers, and hides, which formed its only wealth. In 1816 a great flood bore along the trees that had been left cut upon its banks, and with them made a bar upon its mouth. This bar still exists, and will most probably remain there until the Americans go and open it to their profit. Until this takes place a district, most richly endowed by nature, will remain robbed of half its population, and only half way utilized.

The bay of Nipe extends out into an area of 712 square leagues, deep up to its shores, easy of access and well protected. It is one of the most beautiful as well as the best bays in the world. Thanks to its position on the northern coast, and the advantages before detailed, it could become one of the best markets in the Island. But now its fertile and smiling shores do not present to the sight of the admiring traveller other than a small cultivated district, which is called Mayari, and is situated on the river of that name. There is no road which leads out into the green belts surrounding it, and the port has not been habilitated. What does this barbarous world signify? That it is closed to commerce.

And what of popular education! It hardly exists in the country and in the towns. To open schools for the free colored imposes heavy sacrifices. These schools which the Councils furnish, and whose expenses they propose to defray, dèrive much more money from associations of beneficence, called *Sociedades Economicas de Amigos del Pais*. The proportion of persons who can read, excepting the slaves, is greater in Cuba.than in the provinces of the Peninsula Iberica. (Informacin sobre Reformas). And in what respect does the government lends its aid? In no wise. It simply favors it with Platonic stimulants, and as the Councils have been shorn of the greater part of their resources by the decree of the 12th of February, 1867, the greater part of the schools are going to be closed for want of teachers. In effect these as well as the professors in the institutes of the second class schools have had no money, it is now 18 months, and the *Diario de Cuba* of the 18th of March, written under the eye of the censor, represents them as without shoes or clothing, dead of hunger, annoyed by implacable creditors, and obliged to look to other resources for an honorable means of living. Would it not be supposed from this, that the government is negligent in the matter of literature? I refer to the testimony of a respectable member of the city council of Guantanamo, who lately said to me: "Our municipality received, it is now two years, an official communication from the governor of this department," the tenor of which was: The Most Excellent Senor Governor Superior Civil, recommends to all the councils the purchase of the important work of Dr. Lanuela, because of its practical utility in the country, for the practise of medicine in private families.

The consequence is, that the city council of Guantanamo ought *to subscribe for r respectable number of copies for distribution among the laboring men. The Governor of the Eatern Department, Juan Jose del Villar." The cost was $200. The same recommendation was repeated with reference to the "magnificent work of Dr. Villalon" on Agriculture.

Moreover, what is that which the state favors? The religion, Catholic, apostolic, Romauic, without doubt? Yes, not that she ruins herself in founding parishes, for the country needs both churches and pastors, nor in disseminating religious instruction among the masses. Certain good regulations have been published, which are not, however, observed. A few Draconian laws which are, happily, not regarded· at all. Good examples are given by paying profusely the high dignitaries of the church. For example, the Metropolitan Archbishop of Santiago de Cuba has an income of $18,000 per annum, which he duplicates by subventions—total, $36,000. Poor man! The individual of whom we speak is the Most Excellent, Illustrious, and Most Reverend Senor Doctor Don Such-an-one, most worthy Archbishop of this Diocese. And now, having heard all these titles pronounced, does it not seem that he is indeed well paid? The salary of the Bishop of Havana is, however, larger. The Vicars General, the Canons, the Prebendaries, are paid in proportion. As to the smaller clergy, evangelical poverty is its patrimony, a a little more or less everywhere.

We have said that the government gives a good example. This is a matter of justice due it to say. Every traveler who passes through Cuba on St. James' day, can see the patron of Spain, with cap and sword, mounted on horseback, passing through the streets, followed by a brilliant cortege, in which figure all the authorities, civil, religious, and military. In the same way, on Holy Friday, the Captain-General, at Havana, and his representatives in the other points of the isle, make it a duty to follow the image of the Mother of Sorrows, whose bosom is

---

* Nearly all the Corporations have titles; The City Council of Havana is *Most Excellent* Besides those of the large towns are called *Most Illustrious*, while *Illustrious* is applied to the Councils of the smaller places. If Spain does draw a sufficient sum of money, she gives back at least a good number of titles.

pierced by a sword. These go in procession, heads uncovered, and tapers in hand. On the week of Pentecost, we have seen the troops conducted, for four consecutive days, to mass, the first three being in honor of the Holy Spirit, and the last for Saint Anthony, of Padua. A third part of the year is made up of fête days, whose observance is prescribed by the civil law ; and, as the church does not grant enough, to these have been added numerous political holidays. In the last monarchy, there were six of these : two in honor of " our bounteous Queen," two for the King, and two for the Heir Presumptive. The negroes have their fête days likewise ; among these are numbered that of St. Christina. The country not only loses the money that would have been made by labor on these feast days, but spends, besides, a great deal of means already accumulated." We are ruined by the holidays—one injures the other, and the priest of some new saint adds forever more to his cash-box.*

Besides, the government occupies itself in avoiding the poison of heresy, the proof which is to be found in Article 1st of the royal order of 1817, always in full force. Strangers, subjects of foreign nations, who come to establish themselves in the Island of Cuba, should swear that they profess the religion, Catholic, Apostolic and Roman, and without this indispensable condition they will not be permitted to domicil themselves. †

The rules of *governacion and police* say in the first article: " Sundays and days of precept will be observed, as prescribed by our Holy Mother Church," and in the second article ; When the Viaticum or Host is met in the streets every one should get down upon his knees, and those on horseback and in carriages should descend in order that they may do the same."

---

* On the 10th day of June, 1868, "El Redactor," the periodical official of the Eastern Department, distributed an extra, divided into two columns. In the first, there were the words: "Official.—The procession of the most holy Corpus Christi, suspended because of bad weather, will take place on to morrow, Sunday, the 14th, at 6 o'clock in the morning." In the second, there was this announcement : "Royal Lottery of the Ever Faithful Island of Cuba. The largest premiums." (Here follows the list of the premiums.)

† Or swear that within two years they will become Catholics. Note of translator.

V.

The government protects, likewise, commerce, but in the interests of Spain, though without much benefit, as the letter of General Dulce, written to the Minister of the Colonies, in 1867, declares: "The cause of trouble and of the inquietude which oppresses the Island of Cuba should be sought for to a great extent in the tariff laws, which, under pretext of protection, make impossible a commerce carried on in good faith, render sluggish commercial and maritime movements, foster fraud, as well as make impossible a legitimate commerce, under which said aspects both national and colonial interests suffer. The custom-house system is very expensive, overloaded with formalities which do not impede fraud, but which embarrass and annoy honest trade. The ordonnance of *matriculas*, in lieu of protecting industry upon the seas, has well nigh destroyed it, and in an Island where the multitude and excellency of its ports are well known, there are to be found numerous keys on the coast which afford large facilities for coasting and fisheries."

Notwithstanding the number and excellence of its ports, of which General Dulc speaks, only fifteen are used for commercial purposes on a coast of 560 leagues in extent. Wherefore? Because the others are not opened.

Spain has reserved the monopoly of flour in Cuba to the farmers of Castile by the aid of an enormous differential duty. From this it results that bread, aliment of the first necessity among every civilized people, and especially those of the Latin race, has been converted into a luxury, and is placed beyond the reach of the poor; for a pound of bread is sold at about twelve pence. The population of the Island in round numbers is about 1,400,000 souls; the consumption of flour annually is 75,000,000 lbs., according to the last statistics. The result is that each inhabitant consumes 53 lbs. 9 oz. the year, while in Spain the consumption is 400 lbs. for each individual. Here is a people condemned to live without bread for the greater benefit of the agriculturists of Castile. If the disposition should be felt to make the most of this monopoly, yet whole years pass occasionally as in the last, in which there is found to be more money gained by consuming the flour in Spain or in sending it off to the rest of Europe, and not sending any to Cuba ; there resulting in this way a protection which has nothing to protect, and a monopoly which has nothing upon · which to use its power. As to the United States Cuba cannot ask of them provisions, for since 1844, by way of reprisals for the excessive duties levied by Spain, the Union determined : 1st. That every Spanish ship which comes to the United States shall·give bond in double the amount of the cargo taken on board. 2nd. That vessels coming from Cuba, over and above the differential duties common to the flags of all nations, shall pay an additional duty equivalent to the duty imposed in Cuba between the national and American flags.

If at any time the Castilians send their flour to Cuba, where a similar foreign product pays a differatial duty of $3 20 per barrel of 200 lbs. in exehange, they do not receive our products except by the payment of an enormous tax for the privilege of entry, which in 1863, amounted for the Island of Cuba and Porto Rico, so high as 208,257,339 reals vellon, say : $10,412,866 91. The duties of entry are so high, that only sugars of a superior quality can be imported into Spain, for no one thinks of intro. ducing the inferior qualities, their selling price being only the one half, they are made to pay the same duty. The truth is, that these enter the Peninsula by way of France and Germany after being refined in those countries. Thus it is understood in Spain how protection is given to its sugar refineries.

The result is that whileSpain through her colonies is the greatestproducer of sugars, she is the smallest consumer of them, according to the statistics found in the *Diccoinary of Commerce and Navigation*, which gives the consumption of sugars for each inhabitant in the different countries during the period of 1856 to 1859. She figures in the last rank even after the Roman States and the Government of Naples, at the rate of 760 grammes for each inhabitant, while England figures in the list at the rate of 15 kilogrammes, 136 grammes. If Spain would deign to lower her tarriffs, Cuba would sell her sugars, because there would then be more demand, and it is even probable that the government would gain by the operation. That which has been said with respect to sugars can be repeated as to coffee and cocoa ; as to tobacco, it follows that the Island has to struggle with the State monopoly. Thus we see the proportion in which the tobacco of Cuba is used in Spain compared with that which is received from other countries. For the year 1862 and in the first six months of 1863, there entered for consumption according to an official statement : Tobacco from Cuba, 5,105,664 lbs., Phillipines, 5,286,876 lbs., from foreign countries, 27,215,606 lbs. ; that is to say, 73° of tobacco from other countries against 27° raised in its own colonies. In this manner the Spaniards are condemned by the fisc to use a tobacco of inferior quality when they have colonies which produce the finest tobacco in the world. What do we see in all this ? That the ships of Bremen and Hamburg come to Cuba for the purpose of loading tobacco in leaf, which is to be worked up abroad, and afterwards to be sold in the United States and Europe as Havana tobacco.

The government has other means of favoring maratime commerce : for example, by obliging coasting steamers to transport its employees, its soldiers and effects, upon the presentation of an order from the treasury, which will pay when it can. Since the war, this protection has increased. This caused ships to be presented to the government, which are afterwards armed, or, at least are diverted from their regular course of service in order that troops may be transported, cannons, amunitions of war, and these are paid for by a letter rendering thanks to the proprietor for the *gratuitous* service he has rendered the state. The merchant who receives this attentive recognition, proposes to himself, though it may be somewhat late to do so, that he will not again be thus used ; but in fifteen days the same request is made, and this is always followed by a prompt obedience—in spite of all reclamations. Lucky is, indeed, the party fitting out if, by reason of dullness, his vessel be not sunk, as was the case with the " El Cobrero."

I reserve space within which to speak of the gavel duties, and the exactions without number which weigh upon the country. Here I will not cite more than one in which commerce suffers particularly. Every letter which the French and English steamers bring, though paid abroad, pays here 1fc—25c.,and those coming from the United States, 12½c.*   The journals and pamphlets pay more still, in proportion, and are calculated arbitrarily, according as they may come by the mail from Havana or Santiago de Cuba.   The amount varies, even to doubling itself, but is never less than 1 real fuerte, 63 centimes of a franc (12½ cents.)   And you need not suppose that the letters and papers are going to be carried to your residence.   It is necessary to go and ask for them at the post-office; and, if not, an additional 12 centimes (12½ cents) is to be paid to the carrier.   In vain has commercial men cried out against this gavel tax, which is onerous all the year round.   Never has the slightest concession been obtained. Spain has taken care while celebrating postal treaties with France, to exclude her colonies from their benefits; and she is surprised that these colonies now would like to get rid of the union!   Add to all these things, so agreeable as they are, the most detestible of mony systems which, because of an exact relation between silver and gold, makes us pay more dearly and sell at cheaper rates in our negotiations abroad and with Spain. This phenomenon is due to the fact, that an imaginative value is given to gold of 6¼ per cent more than its actual weight—the object being solely, it is said, to keep it in the country.   This is achieved, in fact, but the same process carries off all the silver.

The administration, desiring to remedy this evil, increased the value of fractional money (1827 to 1840) to 25 per cent.   Silver ran as a sheep, while the gold fiew away.

Twenty cent pieces were again brought down to their true value; but as gold values were unchanged, silver went down the same track by which it had come up, and it became necessary to have recourse to foreign moneys (silver), which, fixed at a rate lower than was the Spanish value, lost nothing by entering into

---

* Even more is paid. Letters which come from Jamaica and Mexico, pay 2fc.---5c0.

relations with over-valued gold. American money arrived, but
not in a sufficient quantity ; and hence a stimulus was given to
French franc pieces (20 cents), and the five cent American pieces
were received at par—that is to say, for five cents—and these
were introduced into commerce with a real French vivacity.
Commerce manifested a disquietude at this overloading speculation, and refused to receive the 20 centime pieces, except at one-
half of what they had been taken. There was a crisis in the
bodegas (provision stores), and among the lower people. Now,
the authorities intervened, saying, " Restless as is the most Excellent Captain-General and Governor Superior Civil for the
wellbeing of the people, he has decided that the 20 centime
pieces of French money shall continue to pass for 5 cents in the
smaller classes of commerce." The merchants rose against this
order of the Captain-General, who, ever indefatigable and never
erring, launched forth another decree, reducing the value of the
piece to 4 cents. But the panic had commenced, and no one was
willing to take it at this price. The Head Authority, surprised
because of his not being able to control the money market as a
camp, reiterated the orders, supporting them by heavy fines and
imprisonment. He did not succeed in this, and the speculation
was charged with shipping these moneys back the way whence
they had come.

VI.

" Agriculture is the stomach of States," said Sully. Let us
see how Spain treats this organ. The isle of Cuba counts 831,281
freemen and slaves devoted to agricultural labors—that is to
say of the three-fourths parts of the fixed population, and pays
consequently, the three-fourth part of the taxes. These ascended
in 1867 to $32,882,253, according to the last statistics. The net
product of rural property amounted to $38,032,502, which, in
proportion to the three-fourth part of the tax, pays, consequently,
$24,661,639. Add to this the fact that the tax is paid nearly

---

* Decree 27th August, 1868.

always by anticipation, and agriculture, it will be seen, pays not exactly upon the taxes, but upon the *expectation* of the taxes. Hence, the necessity of asking a loan, of making a contract of *refaccion*, which is the same thing ; a necessity so much the more prejudicial, as the interest of the money is superior to that which the lands produce. That precious territory, known to the smokers of the whole world, and which possesses many natural ports whence all its products might be commodiously shipped, is obliged to transport them by means of mules, tracing routes which have no name, and rivers, even, up to the *opened* port. This is not all. Commerce of importation and exportation can not be carried on in the same territory, and the *vegueros* find themselves compelled, in order to have objects of prime necessity, to submit to the law of the laboring population, which provides a credit based upon the next crop, and obtains for them money upon the same guarantees at an usurious rate, as high as from eighteen to twenty-four per cent. " The truth is, and is important to be known," say the delegates to Madrid in 1866, "that the principal Cuban product, sugar, causes at present a loss to those who devote their time and capital to it. The proprietors of estates are nothing more than simple administrators of property, the products of which are absorbed by taxes and usury. Let the mortgage offices be examined, and we shall see the different failures which daily occur." In an extensive and judicious report presented to the Captain-General by Don Juan Poey, one of the largest proprietors in the Island, it has been demonstrated from the best ascertained facts, that, taking into account the total production of sugar in the country, there is an annual loss of $1,340,117, which is divided among the 1,365 sugar estates, or 487–1000 per cent. on the capital employed, and this interest without taking into account the cost of insuring the machinery, houses, &c., the epidemics to which the negroes are subject as well as animals, nor the deterioratien of capital employed on the lands, the establishments and machinery. If we pass over from sugar to tobacco, whose cultivation is in the second degree the nerve of our agriculture, and the base of a very rich export, we see with alarm and pain that it moves off to other districts. . . . Coffee, a principal source of abundant and valuable commerce in a day not far behind us, succumbed at last to the blows of our economical and tax-gathering legislation, so much so as that the question is now being raised whether there shall be enough made for our own consumption. And thus disconsolate, let us cut off from view this decadence of our richest agricultural industries in order to fix it upon those more modest, though not less important ones which give life and occupation to the most rural of our population, where poverty, frequently misery, with all its suite of ills annexed presents itself to us in all its horrible nakedness. Thus we shall be convinced that there exists a profound disturbance, in all the elements that go to make up the country wealth of Cuba, much stronger than the efforts of science or the will of those who till the soil, and which cannot be remedied by more hands, with which it is pretended to combat it. (Informacion sobre Reformas). What, then, are the disturbing elements that cause these evils? Before all others, slavery! A short calculation is sufficient to demonstrate that the production of slave, is dearer than that of, free labor.

Let us suppose an estate which needs 300 hands ; if the work be done by free labor, calculating the price at half a dollar per day for each hand, and fixing the number of work days at 250 during the year, which is the largest number employed in agricultural labor, the proprietors will have to pay out $37,500. But the Cuban estate owners, in order to have 300 day laborers must employ at least 350 slaves, for from this number a deduction must be made for the old, infirm and children. These slaves at the moderate price of $500 each, represent a capital of $175,000 ; they must be lodged, fed, taken care of, clothed and even baptized and buried, that which cannot be done except at an outlay of money ; so that, even supposing the expenses of keeping them is equal to the one half of the free laborers, who cannot cost less than $31,937 to the proprietor at the end of 365 days, which sum added to the interest of $17,000 at 10 per cent., makes $49,437*, the result is $11,397 more than in the first case sup-

---

* The interest is supposed to be 10 per cent., but the common rate is 12 per cent.

posed, and which did not involve the necessity of employing a capital of $175,000.

In the first case the sugar planter does not need more than $37,500 for carrying on his establishment; in the second he needs $175,000+$31,937=206,000. The consequence of this excess of capital in the production is to make it exceedingly costly and possible only when products of great value, such as sugars, coffee, and tobacco are to be raised; and even then their price in the market are such as that they are in a poor condition to meet the same sorts of products coming from other countries. To these evils, which harrass agriculture, there is to be added the excessive cost of articles of consumption and handicraft (provisions, sausages, clothing, instruments, &c.) which come from abroad, and are taxed when imported by a heavy duty at the custom-house and a direct tax likewise, at 14 per cent.; so that the production is found to fall in exceptional conditions, and the producers in the road to bankrutcy.

It is not alone by reason of the great amount of capital employed that the cost of production is increased; it is by reason of the inferiority of slave labor. Senor Poey, planting himself upon the official statistics, has demonstrated that with a middling force of 145 laborers, an estate makes 1887 boxes of middling product whilst the experiences and example of foreign colonies show that 64 laborers aged from 10 to 60 years, are sufficient to the production. From which there results are an excess of 71 laborers, who at a valuation of $800 each, the mean price of an adult slave, necessiates the employment of an unproductive capital of $56,800 on each estate. The inferiority of servile labor results from ignorance, from the want of enterprise and the absence of emulation on the part of the laborers, and those defects, in their turn, throw their influence back upon the proprietor, keeping him in the same routine and hindering agricultural progress in which there must be some intelligence with the laborer. So it happens that there is not to be seen in Cuba none of those new industrial proceedings of which the Americans make such admirable use, and which are adapted to all kinds of farm labor from the rude work of felling timber to the delicate process of sowing seed, of the cultivation, and in gathering of the crop. There are no sawing machines to cut up the giants of the forest, no apparatus to draw up the roots from the earth, no steam machines, no plows to break up the virgin soil; no machines to sow or to plant, no scythes to cut the cane as is done by wheat and hay. All this is done by muscular force, with instruments of the most primitive kind. This requires more men and animals, and, as a matter of course more capital with less product. The scanty profit of slave labor, united to the cheapnes and abundance of land, has conduced to a system of cultivation in which there is asked from the soil that which cannot be exacted from imperfect labor. For this reason we see agriculture obliged to seek new land, because of the sterility which comes upon those already opened by reason of ignorance, thus abandoning considerable capital and leaving behind devastation and desert places. The cultivation looses in intensity what it gains in extensiveness. According to Don Juan Poey, the mean extent of the estate is equal to 42¼* caballerias of land, the value of which does not fall below $63,-510, and which ought to render a product of 2,109 arrobas per each caballaria, nothwithstanding in Jamaica and Bengal a sugar estate, mean rendering is estimated at 5,755 arrobas, in the Reunion 7,425 arrobas ; in Barbadoes and in English Guiana, 9,609 arrobas. "Undoubtedly," remarks he, "none of the colonies have better lands than Cuba, but free labor, which has taken place of slave labor, permits a use of means more perfect. If the cultivation of the cane had been so far advanced as in Barbadoes and Guiana, 9,29–00 caballarias of land would give the same amount of sugar as the 42½ caballarias before mentioned, and in the installation of this estate of 9,29–00 callebrias there would be saved $44,575, the interest of which at the lowest rate, 9 per cent., would have a tendency to reduce the general expenses."

The remedy, one would say, is easy : "Give liberty to the slaves, and call them freemen." That is just what is desired by the intelligent men of the country; that is what was vainly de-

---

* The caballeria is equal to 3 hectares, 42 areas, about 33¼ acres. La arrobas.—25 lbs.

manded by the delegates of Cuba and Porto Rico, at Madrid, in in 1866. By a Michaelivan policy, Spain is forced to preserve slavery, that she may oppose the brutal elements of the negro race to the legitimate aspirations of the white race. This is what the profound statesmen of Spain have honored with the expression—*equilibrium* of the races in the island of Cuba. We give place to the statement of the representatives of Cuba to the government in 1866, to the end that the reader may see on which side is the wrong, and where should rest, according to impartial history, the opprobrium of preserving slavery up to this good day.

" We protest," said they, " in the most solemn manner against the theory of a commission of government, which, up to yesterday even, had not indicated the equilibrium of the races in Cuba as a means of order and conservatism, thus giving a sad proof of its political designs, and of its love for civilization! If we be told that only the black and yellow races are capacitated by nature for agricultural labor in a tropical climate—that the severity of this labor and the rigors of that climate, as well as its moderate cost, will be always a powerful obstacle to white emigration, we reply : This argument is not new. It has been made from the time of the conquest, and has ever had a support in the ignorance and avarice, which brought about the slave trade as well as slavery."

Not to speak of the great number of agents, of engineers. of employeees, European an American in origin, and who are engaged upon the *ingeuos*, the labor on ports, streets, quarries and railroads is done almost wholly by white labor.

More than this ; not only a great number of emigrants prefer agriculture on a small scale and for their own proper account as the Vizcainos and Gallegos, but there is a great number of employés, upon salaries, in the great fabrics considered, up to the present, as worked by negroes and Chinese. The official statistics number 41,621 whites employed on estates. Don Juan Poey, upon the authority of figures furnished by Dr. Artenor Betancourt, Regidor de Holquin, tells us that in 1861 there were in that jurisdiction three small estates worked exclusively by whites, and there are now in the Island 200 small farms on which canes are grown and sugar made. In Cuba the statistics prove that of the 793,484 whites (1861) 454,597 were devoted to agriculture. This demonstrates, likewise, that of the total of the agricultural population, being 853,242, 53⅓ per cent. is white, 12½ per cent. free colored, and 34⅓ are slaves; proportions which are fruitful of reflection.

The progressive increase of the white population in the Island which has mounted since 1795 from 86,440 to 793,484—does it not prove the emptiness of the statement that the climate hinders emigration and the increase of the white race? What would be the consequence, if instead of being impeded, emigration were fostered and stimulated? Why is it not larger? Because the laborers find their places occupied by the negroes and Chinese; because of the gloom inseparable from the system of slavery which degrades and renders vile all labor, dispenses with intelligence and suppresses the free will of the laborer, rendering him a docile and inert instrument of the will of another, inaugurating thus in Cuba a brutal and destructive system of agriculture, which, at the same time, that it wastes the soil, ruins the generations of laborers, sacrificing unnumbered victims to its avarice. In vain would it be to counsel the Cubans to reform their agriculture, as though it were not necessary to make a change in order to avoid henceforth a heap of obstacles foreign to science and the art of agriculture, and independent of its action and will. As if agriculture did not have a foundation in the very vitals of that society in which it was cradled, and as if it were thrown out of accord with the institutions which direct it.

Agriculture, the object of which is the production of riches—can it get along without roads, rivers, and maritime communications, is it independent of the market situation, of commercial treaties, of the regimen of the custom-house, of the credit system, of the security of things and persons, of the administration of justice, of municipal management, as well as of provincial, of public instruction, in a word, of all the elements which combine to form the government of a society? To pretend to better or to transform agriculture in the midst of immutable exterior conditions, of sedentary institutions, of elements economo-political which do not favor it, is to betray an ignorance of its nature and its laws.

To transform of itself a system of agriculture, which to-day owes its deplorable condition (as we have explained) to these same causes, and to the mode of governing, which has brought it about, overwhelmed by a mortgage debt, which represents nearly the whole of its fixed capital, and the interest on which absorbs the greater part of the current production ! . . . . to transform itself, in spite of a concurrence of exterior causes, of the most active kind, punished in its better markets by the system of reprisals originating out of our hard customs' tariffs ; forced to sell at the lowest prices, to the end that articles of its own consumption and elaboration may be purchased at an extra price of at least 30 per cent. . . . . to transform it, when guarentees and security in the interior are wanting, without streets and neighborhood roads, without institutes of learning of a primary class or schools wherein it may be taught, subject as they are to the abuses and arbitrary conduct of the lesser authorities and its moral agents. . . . . which pays more than 75 per cent of the enormous tax of $32,852,223, to which is to be added nearly 18 per cent on the crude, and of 48 per cent on the net product." . . . transform it, no ; to transform it would be to ruin it completely, because there would be nothing left ; it would not tend to put it in a condition to undertake the bettering of it in the way which science indicates.

To this end, nothing resembling the slave trade, nor the introduction of Chinese, which is a masked slave trade, is worth anything. That which is necessary is the suppression of embarassments in the custom house ; the abolition of injustice in the public administration, as well as its reparation; a politic as well as economical legislation, which would diminish our expenses of production, increase the number of our markets, and raise the price of our products. Thus will an agricultural transformation be obtained of itself, for the improvements and guarantees which flow from such a system, would give to agriculture the means of buying new instruments, to increase the pay of dependents, to adopt new methods,—in a word, to bring about all those conditions within which all kinds of labor would be multiplied.

" Let Spain bring about, in fine, (for her honor and our good,) the abolition of slavery, without a compromise of material interests, or a violation of any acquired right—that is to say, by progressive emancipation, and within a fixed time. This would be the best stimulus for the emigration of the white race." *Informacion Sobre Reformas en Cuba y Porto Rico.* Such were the just demands of the representatives of Cuba and Porto Rico. But the Spanish government was but little disposed to condescend to grant that which was asked for by the inhabitants of the Antilles.

In the meeting which took place on the 6th of December, 1866, between the delegates of the Antilles and the government commissioners, Senor Angulo, a representative from the city of Mantanzas, made a motion to declare the slave trade piracy, with all the consequences resulting therefrom. Senor San Martin, a representative from Havana, said on this occasion, " that it was necessary to Spanish honor that the trade should be declared piracy,—that the monarchy had lost its presitige before the nations of Europe, that we had been lying in the face of the world, and that it was proper to confess with shame that the treaty had been carried on solely because of the tolerance of the government."

The motion was voted by the majority, only three members being opposed to it, of whom one was a senator, another a priest, who excused himself by saying that his sacred office impeded the giving of his approbation to a means which involved the death penalty ; the other was an old minister of colonial affairs, who opposed the measure frankly. All the three were elected by the government, and commissioned by it to treat of colonial reforms in connection with those chosen by popular suffrage.

The committee named in consequence to take into consideration this motion, truly exposed the situation by saying, " It is sufficient that a *capiain del partido* is willing to let an expedition be landed, to have the thing done. How, in effect, can this

officer resist him who says : ' Take ten, fifteen or thirty thousand
dollars without receipt, silent and unobserved, which you may
keep for yourself. I only ask that on to-morrow morning, instead of being here, you may be in some other part of your jurisdiction ? ' " The Lieutenant-Governors, likewise, wink at the
landing of these expeditions, because there is considerable money
to be made, and a sense of honor is not strong enough to prevent
their being seduced. The thing is to attain it in this case by the
heroism of honor, and frankly as heroes are not common, and are
exacting, however they may seem, (and particularly so to me, who
look upon them as adventurers,) the true reason is reached which
explains the constant permission accorded by the authorities to
the landing of these negro expeditions ; and whatever means
may be adopted, I believe will, in truth, continue to exist here-
after. " Demoralization has reached the extreme point—that is,
understandings and pre-arrangements are had with respect to
this kind of business, and it has even happened that the public
functionaries and employees of the government—those charged
with enforcing its orders and causing the laws to be respected,
have worked zealously to the end that landings *might* be effected
in their own jurisdictions, thus taking means to prove their own
complicity in the matter, and getting a good reward as the price
of their prevarication and dishoner."

"To invent the theory of equilibrium of races—this supposes that the Spaniards born in Cuba . . . . were for the mere
reason of having seen the light there, determined enemies of
their fathers . . . whom it were not possible to restrain without
pouring in a constant horde of people antagonistic and semi-
savage." This doctrine having been made to embrace the slave-
trade there was nothing to be done but to implore condescen-
ion : the upraised head of slavery, in effect said that he was a
bad Spaniard who aspired to hinder the prevention of the national integrity by an equilibrium of races.

A man generally esteemed, counsellor Antonio G. de Mendoza
thought of forming an association somewhat like the temper-
ance societies in form, in which men would give their word of
honor not to buy negroes introduced into the Island of Cuba
after the 19th of November, 1863.

This project was authorized by General Dulce, but the Metropolitan government disapproved it and left it *provisional*, by putting the matter in the hands of the Superior Chief of the Island. Now returning to the committee, of which we speak, its labors were concluded by asking. 1st. That the trade should be declared piracy ; 2nd. That the purchasers of negroes, *bozales* or Africans, should be considered as accomplices in piracy ; That the anti-slave-society, the character of which was pacific and inoffensive, should command the approbation of the government.

None of these conclusions were adopted, nor were they submitted to the deliberation of the Cortes Constituyentes. It is not sufficient to assimilate the slave trade to piracy, it is necessary to wound it in the heart by abolishing slavery itself. Why was it that Spain for her own good, as well as ours, did not accept the plan of emancipation proposed, gradual in character, and which would have required 7 year's time for consummation ? This conceded $450 to the proprietor for each slave between the ages of seven and sixty years ; the indemnity to be paid by the Island, and without costing Spain a dollar, asking of her only a fair and equitable tariff of duties. It was calculated that the total subvention for the owners of slaves would amount to $50,000,000, which the Island would have paid in seven years, without even increasing the scale of taxes, and which would have been withdrawn from the articles now unjustly made to pay duties. This is precisely what Spain did not wish to do.

Imagine all the infamy that the institution of slavery engenders ! As in the shadow of the poisonous Manchinelle tree there grow and conceal themselves envenomed grasses, so the shadow of slavery has given birth to the bastard stem, called *emancipation.* This name is given to the negroes who come out in ships caught in Cuban waters since the international treaty was made with reference to the trade. The government seizes these and then delivers them up for a certain quantity of money, or hires them in a sum which varies more or less on according to the good will of the Captain-Generarls, and his particular friends, who become masters for the space of eight years. Those who are born of emancipated parents, before the latter shall have obtained their free papers, become slaves of the government for 25 years, at least such is the the law; but in parctice the *emancipados*, as a general thing, wait al their lives for their free papers.

In 1867 an order from Madrid was given that all the *emancipados* who had fulfilled the eight years should be set at liberty, unless they desired tor remain with their patrons; but this order was delayed in the matter of being carried into execution.

I saw in 1867, at Santiago de Cuba, one of these unhapy men, whowished to redeem himself as an ordinary slave at $700 or $800, accumulated by sweat and privations; the authorities (as ball-players), terrified him *a la pelota* in order to fix his position, which they could not do, because the disposition as to freedmen was not applicable to an *emaneipatdo*.

Public opinion is, that in all epochs, the governors and other high functionaries have enriched themselves with the hires of the *emancipades*, whose number the government at Madrid could never ascertain. "During my stay at Havana, says D'Harponville, pp. 279," the same wife of the Captain-General had for her earnings men of this class whom she hired out at $15 and $16 per month." An author, already cited, Senor Galiano, who was for a long time director of the officious journal, the *Diario de la Mamia*, says in his book (Cuba in 1858). "With a little more condescension and flexibility in the back-bone, means of utitliy which I recognize though I do not practice, I could vegetate in peace, and even make use of my dozen *emancipados*."

But this is nothing in comparison with the criminal abuse which is dealt out by piecemeal with respect to the persons of these unfortunates. They are made to pass for dead by means of certificates of interment, easily obtained. Or, when a negro of the estate dies, the *euancipado* is reported dead, to whom the name of the dead slave is given in the meantime.

It is not so easy to play the same game with the Chinese; but what shall we say of the Draconic regulations which control them? The contract once terminated, they are obliged to enter into a new one or return to their country at their own cost, or to employ themselves on the public works.

Is this not to condemn them to forced labor for their whole
lives? And this regulation does not authorize that theyshall bo
whipped with the thong of a whip, which is used upon the
slaves, but with a club.

If Spain desires the introduction of negroes and Chinese, she
does not wish to introduce whites. The reason has been very
clearly given by some of her statisticians. " Peninsular emigration ought not to be encouraged ; because Spain needs hands,
and that of foreigners should not be fostered, because Spain
cannot bear the idea of losing her dominion in the Antilles." In
this spirit was written the royal order of 1817, which governs in
this particular up to the present.

We well know the provisions of Article 1st. It is necessary
that the party interested should be a Catholic. Conformably to
Article 2d, the oath of fidelity is taken before the Governor, and
that of vassalage also! " Within five years," says Article 3d,
" foreigners should be naturalized or leave the country. In this
last case, they may take away their accumulations ; but conformably to Article 5th, they should abandon one-tenth of their ac-
quisitions. The 18th Article says : "During the first five years
these persons cannot carry on commerce, neither possess a shop,
nor store, nor be captains of vessels ; but they may have an interest in a company or association of Spaniards." Article 22d
has this : " It is declared that the duties under which the government and fisc sequestrate'and take possession of the property
of foreigners, a rule reserved in that which concerns travel-
ers, shall never be applied to persons domiciled." Article 48th :
" Foreigners who have no letter of domicil will be compelled to
leave the island in three months, under penalty of being tried
and punished for disobedience to the law."

Such is the by-law protecting foreign emigration. It is true
that all its requirements are not enforced ; but this alone proves
toleration on the part of the local authorities, and the central
government does not omit to reproduce them in royal orders.
It is not long since General Dulce made pretentions towards
obliging foreigners, resident at Havana, more than five years, to
go through the process of naturalization. When Spain cele-

brates treaties with foreign nations, a provision is always insert-
ed to the effect that her colonies are not to be included in their
provisions. So declares the Royal Order of 25th of August,
1846, another of 5th August, 1847, and, in fine, the international
treaty with France, in 1862, as well by the cedula (order) of
1817, as by all the dispositions posterior. Foreigners are subjected to all the inconveniences possible. But again ; should a
foreigner become naturalized, does he acquire the favor of the
administration ?

A distinguished publicist, a worthy magistrate, known to the
reader, Dr. Vincente Vazquez Quipo, will enlighten us as to this.
According to him the founder of Cienfuegos, to-day one of the
most flourishing towns in the Island, died in misery. He was a
Frenchman, a naturalized Spaniard, who was called Don Louis
Declouet, against whom the fisc brought ruinous suits.

" Even though it were true," said the government attorney of
the Royal Treasury, Vasquez Quipo, "that Declouet has realized more advantages than were embraced within the terms of
the colonization contract entered into between him and the government—has he appropriated the $130,000 of revenue which
entered into the Royal Treasury during the past year, and the
products, quadrupled at least, of the new colony, inuring to the
benefit of the public wealth ?

To obtain such results it would not be a good means to bring
against the founders of colonies interminable and ruinous processes for each act done in virtue of the contract of colonization.
The watchfulness of public employees is, indeed, noble ; but of
a truth it has been indiscreet, and, above all, prejudicial to the
public good. Hardly behind what is practiced in our mother
country is this fiscal spirit, which has bargained with foreigners
for the right of establishing themselves in business in the
country, as well as the privilege of bringing here their capital.
The supposition seems to be entertained that they come here to
rob us, as though that which they leave in the matter of knowl-
edge and industry does not avail much more. Who has gained
more in the production of the colony—Fernandina, the Island,
the public treasury, or Clouet ? Would that we had other such

colonies ! but this is not to be looked for ; the example of the colonization of Cienfuegos will prevent other speculators from giving their time to undertakings so full of risk as long as this fiscal spirit exists, wretched as it is, and which has prevailed for so long a time, and forms the base of all the political economy of our government." (Imforme fiscal sobre el fomento de poblacion blanca en la Isla de Cuba. Madrid, 1845.")

VII.

Let us see what an impost the Island of Cuba is taxed with for being so well governed. In 1847 she paid $13,000,000, of which the mother country appropriated $6,000,000. This tribute money is called by the damnable expression, *un sobrante* (a surplus). In 1857 she paid $17,960,000, of which $8,000,000 was raised for Spain. In 1867, the $32,857,233 comprised the pension of Father Claret, which was at the rate of $32 *per capita*, while Spain only paid $7 per head. This progression would seem to indicate an increase of prosperity in the country, but this was not so. In 1857 there was more prosperity than in 1867, there being nearly the same population. In 1857 Spain was at peace with the Sultan of Morocco, with the Emperor of Cochin China, with the Presidents of Mexico, Peru, Chili, and with all the generals of Santo Domingo. Between 1857 and 1867 she had conquered the Moors, fought the Kh-Du in Cochin China, occupied for an instant Vera Cruz, bombarded Valparaiso, cannonaded Callao, and, in fine, had endavored to fasten herself upon Santo Domingo. The increase of taxes in the Island can thus be understood.* In 1868 the imports in Cuba were laid at $43,959,903, but for this time they could not be paid.

---

* The economic year (Spanish), at least that which relates to the Cuban account, commences on the 1st of July, and ends on the 30th of June. Thus, when the year 1868 is spoken of, the time between the 1st of July, 1867, and the 30th of June, 1868, is to be understood. About $30—a real is here five cents.

This result and that which followed had been prognosticated sometime before the insurrection. " I foresee a catastrophe near at hand in case Spain presists in remaining deaf to the just reclamation of the ·Cubans. Look at the old colonies of the American Continent ; all have ended in conquering their independence. Let Spain not forget this lesson ; let the government be just to the colonies that remain. Thus, she will consolodate her dominion over people who aspire only to be good sons of a worthy mother, but who are not willing to live as slaves under the scepter of a tyrant." Don J. A. Saco, delegate from Santiago de Cuba to Madrid, 1866.

The Marquis of O'Gavan, another Cuban, but who being a senator of the kingdom could not be suspected by the government, used the same language. " The provinces over the sea pay 618 reals for each free inhabitant, while those of the Peninsula do not contribute more than 140. The disproportion will be much greater now under the new tributary system imposed upon the Antilles, and had it not been for a mistake in the calculations, the increase would have been $11,000,000. When the affair touches a country overwhelmed with numerous charges which do not appertain to it but to the nation, as for example, the tax for Fernando Po, when by the Mexican and Santo Domingo expeditions, the money (cash) of the bank (capital and deposits) were absorbed and Cuba suffered from this fearful crisis which has mortally injured her credit, it is certainly not the mode to heal up her wounds by opening others." (*Informancom solbe reformas*). All the members of the committee exclaimed with a single voice. "A radical reform in the tributary system is so much the more necessary and urgent when the elevation of imposts has reached a point that cannot be bourne, because they wastes the element of wealth in those beautiful countries." The committee demonstrated by a table drawn up and explanatory of the matter, that the tax for the economic year of '66-'67 exceeded the former one, by $14,780,150. If this proconsular imposts had been properly and economically distributed only one half of the evil would have been done, but it was not so. For example, the custom-houses, for reasons inherent in the social organization of the country and because of the corruption of their employees, presented a schedule of duties so heavy as that it was found necessary either to modify them to a very great extent, or to substitute another in lieu of it.   In a country without industry as Cuba, and which pays almost the whole of the customs, a country of slaves—there is a very small number of proprietors who support all their weight.   In Cuba it may be said, that the rural contribution falls upon 50,000 inhabitants ; the others do not pay anything in comparison with the slaves. Beside the custom-duty is anticipated, and as the owner of slaves sees himself obliged to make great purchases during the year, and as he generally borrows upon his crop the custom-duties doubly press upon him.   Such is the interest ills of the system. And what shall we say of those which spring out of the mode by which they are adjusted and collected.   It is notorious that at Havana fraud and contraband amounts to 40 per cent., and in Santiago de Cuba of 70 per cent.*   From this one can judge that which happens in points less is watached by the superior authority, and where scandalous fortunes are made in a short time by employees who have not refrained, while exercising their functions, from living in an ostentacious style.   While speaking to the reader of the concessions and prevarications of employees of every class and category, I will rely upon the best authority in the matter, to wit : the Attorney of the Royal Treasury.   " The employees," says Vasques Queipo, " who have served in the island of Cuba upon small salaries, compared to the want of supplies in the country, insult, when in Spain, the honest poverty of the employees there, rivaling, as they do, in luxury and property, the nobility itself of the highest class, and even the most august personages."†   The audacity of the custom house employees rose to such a point in Sto. de Cuba, in these last times, that the state collected hardly anything.   It is not solely in the maratime customs where these frauds are committed, but, also, *in the administration of the country taxes* !   Thus the collector, charged with the collection of tax upon incomes, with reason or

---

*Informacion sobre Reformas, tomo 1ª, page 243.

† Information Fiscal, p. 193.

without it, supposes that the proprietor confesses less than what
he should; and, to avoid any difficulty, the proprietor hastens
to pay, without taking any receipt therefor, the one-half of the
difference found between his calculation and that of the collector. It is unnecessary to mention that this one-half never enters
into the cash-box of the state. Whenever a plantation is sold,
the administrator of the landed tax ought to go to where he may
meet the proprietor, in order that he may be assured of the
number of his slaves. But the proprietor and the administrator
have an understanding, thus avoiding the journey by means of
a certificate—which is paid for according to the value of the
property. As large properties are treated as small estates, it is
easy to understand how great a sum must necessarily be derived
from this exaction in a year.

The delegates for Cuba had reason for asking a reform of the
tributary system, ruinous and demoralizing as it is. They
asked, in order that this cancer of immorality might be extir-
pated, that the custom houses should be suppressed, and all the
exactions practised in connection with them—the gavels, vexa-
tions, extortions; and that there might be substituted in lieu, a
fixed tax, which ought to be about six per cent on the net income,
and which would be sufficient to cover the expenses of the estimates.

The answer of the government was not delayed. On the 13th
of February, 1867, that is to say, a month after the report of the
delegates, there appeared in the Official Gazette, a royal decree,
reforming the tributary system. The custom houses were not
suppressed, but there appeared a direct tax of 14 per cent upon
incomes! Let us understand aright these innovations. The
tax had been established in this way upon the income of real
property, on commercial, industrial and professional enterprizes,
in such a manner that nothing, except the churches and property
of state escaped the fixed tax—ten per cent net of which was
destined for state purposes, and four per cent for the municipalities. The delegates from Cuba and Porto Rico protested against
such an enormous contribution, "after having demonstrated,"
said they, "from official figures, that a tax of six per cent on

net incomes would be sufficient to cover the necessities of the
estimates, how can it be figured out that the government, making
a mixed report upon the old and new systems combined, should
not interfere with the custom houses, notwithstanding all their
inconveniences, but establish a direct tax of fourteen per cent?
At the same time that the Antilles hoped to see the contributions discontinued, the Mother Country adopts a plan by which,
retaining all the annoyances that the custom houses, the duties
differential as between flags and other gavels impose upon commerce, there is added an enormous direct contribution in
the examination of which their representatives neither had a
share, nor did they give their approbation. The truth is, that
$7,355,230 of former imposts have been abolished ; but there re-
mains $24,997,000, which, with the addition of ten per cent upon
taxable wealth, ought to raise the sum to $43,959,903—that is to
say, $11,107,670 over and beyond the former estimates,—with-
out counting the estimate municipal. But the delegates were
preaching in a desert ; their commission ended at the moment
when the "reform of the tributary system" had been effected,
and there was nothing left to do but to dismiss them with fine
words, such as these which were used by the Queen : "Love
makes no distinction as between distances. My children in Cuba
and Porto Rico are, in reality, as dear to me as those of the
other provinces." This mode of comprehending love will probably cause the loss of Cuba to Spain.

Without loss of time there was sent out to Havana an able
functionary in order to inaugurate a system of estimates. He
discharged the duty to the satisfaction of the government, if one
were to judge by the honorable distinctions of which he was the
object, but the contributors (tax payers) did not participate in
the enthusiasm, for in place of 14 they found themselves obliged
to pay 18, 21, and even 24 per cent. upon the net income. So
admirable was the exactitude of the calculations, or the honor
which presided over the distribution of the estimates.

The assessors of the taxes in each jurisdiction, in each settle-
ment, in each municipality, were liable to commit errors, or
might perpetrate injustice, but the origin of the evil was, without
doubt, in the faults committed at the treasury, where the sum of

the public wealth was greatly exaggerated, besides the application of the rules for raising the estimates were enforced with a frightful rigor ; the pastry cook, who in his store sold liquors with his cakes, was obliged to pay as a liquor dealer, and as though that was his regular business.

The proprietors of untilled lands had to pay upon them at the same rate as upon the adjoining cultivated fields. The proprietor in such case preferred to abandon his lands, as did also the keepers of country taverns who found themselves in the same condition. The lawyers gave up the practice of their profession in order to escape the tax ! At Bayamo, a poor city of 5,000 inhabitants, five lawyers in a single day gave up their profession. How many remained ? One at least ; too many for Spain : Don Carlos Emanuel Cespedes, to-day President of the Cuban Republic ! Under this system the government instead of collecting $43,000,000, which it expected, was not able to realize the one-half of that sum. There was a reason for persisting in its plan.

Against the expectations of the country this tributary system was continued in full play for the economic year of 1868. Moreover, the head officer of the treasury invented a means of coining money upon the moment without looking to the estimates ; he obliged all the contributors (tax payers) to take out a stamped paper in the office of the administration for their lists, costing 25 cents each, which produced for the treasury an additoinal $25,000

This system of exactionion and taxes, so extravagant as they are, never fails to produce corresponding fruits. The cash of the fisc varies more rapidly than it fills, and it has a horror of emptiness.

The collect of arrears is rigrously recommended with the premiums belonging to their corresponding duties. It seizes upon the oxen of the small laborer with which he tills the soil, or the horse, which serves the poor cattle raiser, used in carrying his vegetables to market. It puts up at public sale the estates of insolvent proprietors, and thus it happens as was the case at Bayamo, there is no bidder, or he is assassinated on the next day. Hence there appeared in the Yara and Bayamo county the banner of insurrection with the inscription, *Long life to Prim, down with the taxes.* As yet there was still hoisted the old flag of Castile. The shells of the Spanish soldiers bore this away, and when it reappeared in the morning of another day, there had been substituted in place of the yellow and red colors of the old Monarchy the red, white and blue of the New State.

Wise economists, illustrious authors of a determined tributary system, you have not read the 8th Satire of Juvenal. " If according your wishes Heaven were to concede to you the goverment of a province limited to your ambitious views, have pity of your own allies and their misery ; they have been chipped away to their marrow bones. Before the situation of our allies were less desolate, piles of dollars where heaped up in in their coffers, and now ? Shall we get hold of them ? Some yoke of oxen, some other animals, . . a miserable field. . . Take care I counsel you; robbery and violence are objects of danger to the brave who suffer. You have wished to take away all their gold and silver; but it is necessary to leave a dollar, the sword and their darts. To the despoiled. . . . That which has been said is not coming from the air, it is an oracle as certain as that of the Sybil.

VIII.

What resources are left for Spanish dominion. The treasury is empty, as much so as the Banco Espanol. The municipal moneys are not sufficient for the many necessities,—as, for instance, the lighting of the streets by gas, the police, the keeping up of hospitals and food for the prisoners. Between the month of October, 1868, and the month of February, 1869, in the capital of the Eastern Department, various individuals, including the alcalde mayor, provided means out of their own pockets for the support of 400 or 500 men in the prisons. On the 30th of September, 1868, the governor of the same department convoked a junta of prominent men in the palace for the purpose of conferring with them with respect to the steps to be taken towards meeting the necessities of the moment, either by voluntary subscriptions or by the levying of new taxes. The city was in debt for gas furnished during the preceding fourteen months; besides it owed nine months' salary to professors of schools of the second class, and seven months' pay to the officers of police.

Nearly all the cities of the island—Mantanzas, Trinidad, Havana, even, were more or less in the same condition, and found themselves obliged to submit to extraordinary sacrifices in order to get along at all. How did this happen, when an additional tax was given them of four per cent by the new law? It is that the administration, which collects the contributions, applies them entirely, even in the matter of the ten per cent, and the municipalities collect the excess. As yet it has been found impracticable to collect the part coming to the State. Those who furnish supplies to the government, under contract, are not paid; and, notwithstanding, they are obliged to fulfill their compromises! In short, the authorities are constantly employing merchant vessels and do pay not the owners for the service rendered.

Such is the situation of the Spanish administration in the presence of the insurrection. There is left no other resource but a well instructed, suffering, but badly-fed soldiery. Will this army be sufficient to preserve Cuba to the Spaniards? This is hardly probable, considering the ruinous state in which the income of the island and of Spain are now found. It is true that something may be, for a time, expected in the way of gifts from the rich Peninsulars of Cuba; but soon these resources will have been wasted, which are put in equilibrium by the sacrifices imposed in a contrary sense, and which the Creoles will continue to impose at any price, with the view of relieving their country of the humiliating and ruinous yoke under which their hopes have, for so many years, been crushed. It is unnecessary to say, that the disciplined troops of Spain are superior to bands wanting in experience, and to recruits who have only come into action since the revolution.

The first has been made so at the expense of the Island of Cuba, and are better armed than the forces in Spain; the second are imperfectly armed, having common guns of chase, and others of all sorts of calibre ; they are without artillery, and are wanting in munitions. But even such as they are their soldiers keep in check $50,000 men ; thanks to the extent of territory and the difficulty of communication ; and of these 30,000 are regular troops. Contraband ministers, though with great difficulty, and in quantities by no means sufficient, to this want. Arms and munitions do arrive, and they will be had in great abundance as soon as the United States shall have recognized the Cubans as belligerents. The generals who commands the Spanish forces are, doubtless, abler men than those who lead the improvised insurgent army, but they have fearful allies, yellow fever and the rainy season. For the first time the Spanish government will regret having left the Island without roads. All this is bad enough without counting upon foreign intervention. In truth, is it a good time for the United States to let such an occasion pass by for causing Spain to lose a prize which the former nation has so much desired? Certainly its intervention in this case would be more plausible than that which was exerted in favor of Juarez in Mexico. Numerous symptoms presage that this intervention will not be looked for in vain for a long time in Cuba.

The party of annexation is not the strongest. Certain highly intelligent persons have experienced a certain inquietude with respect to the results that would follow annexation to the United States. They fear an invasion which would put out of possession the actual holders of the soil, or those coming after them, and that all lucrative branches of industry would be monopolized by others, not by violence, but by the superiority of one race over the other in physical and moral energy, drawn together by the desire of gain.

It is certain that in this struggle for life (battle of life) the advantage would not be in favor of the desendants of the Spaniards, and the *selection* would be at the expense of old possessors. To support this view, Florida, Texas and California are cited. Notwithstanding all this, the Cubans will not retrocede before this extreme view of the subject, and they will end the matter by throwing themselves into the arms ot the Americans. Is this to say that the Cubans are incapable of conquering their independence? No, sooner or later they will aquire it; but I do not think they can preserve it for a long time, as well be cause of their geographical situation as of their neighboring relations; likewise because of the want of political instruction which is common to them as has been the case with all other people emancipated from the dark and smothering dominions of Spain. These considerations are not hidden out of sight by the majority of the Cubans, and for this reason they contented themselves with asking a reform of Spain, which conceded in time, would have saved all. Spain has never wished, either in the past or at this time to concede anything. She contents herself by promising from the mouths of her ministers the concession of reforms (which are not set forth) when the insurrection shall have been quelled. "Not before, answers the interrogator? You have deceived us so often that we do not trust your word." The reply is hard, let us see if it is merited. In 1837, to go no further back Spain, gave herself a very liberal Constitution. It is known for how a small time this was enjoyed; but in any event it was supposed that the Island of Cuba was to have participated in the benefit to flow from the new Constitution, and she was in effect, invited to send deputies to the Cortes to the end that her necessities might be known and her interetss be discussed. Very well; The deputies at the Capital, compelled, a strange thing to say, by the most advanced feaction of the Cortes, refused to receive them, and it was decided that the Island should be governed by special laws, to be enacted by the Cortes in the absence of the legitimate representatives of Cuba. The Cortes had so much to do afterwards that they did not find time to enact these famous laws. Since 1837, that is to say, for a perion of 32 years, the mean rate of human life, the Island of Cuba hoped for the execution of the promise of the Cortes and, in particular, from the liberals of Spain; while expecting it this titanic labor is submitted to the *regimen* of the arbitrary. This is not the occasion to say: "Beautiful Phillis is always in despair when she is always expecting." But so far as the Spanish government is concerned—she never despairs, but rather produces this feeling, on the contrary, when there is taken into account the plenitude of her powers over the Island of Cuba. For example, in 1869, their was a necessity for a law (a thing dealt out in small doses), and not knowing what to borrow money upon she thought of her daughter, the Ever Faithful, The Island of Cuba. A loan of $10,000,000, at 7½ per cent., was negociated, reimbursable in 15 years by successive payments, and to secure this the income of Cuba, Porto Rico, and the Phillippines were pledged for the same number of years. It is certain that the guaranty was sufficient, and a government which finds herself reduced to such a necessity in order to contract a loan under such conditions does not enjoy a wonderful credit.

Notwithstanding the money lenders at length repented, even before commencing to fulfill their compromise. The Spanish liberals in order to damage Narvaez' Administration, gave the buyers to understand that as the Cortes had not voted the loan, it was consequently unconstitutional, and they would incur the risk of having it repudiated by a liberal majority, that which bring about as a result—the total loss of their money.

The discretionary power of Spanish rule in Cuba does not produce barren results. P. Claret knows something of that, for he received 30,000 francs for the part he had in it as a matter of right. Likewise the camarilla (little room) knew something of this, for by it there is sent out upon each change of ministers a set of birds of prey that they may set themselves upon the estimates, linked, as they are, with the New World.

The Creoles compare their country to a green meadow in which the horses of Andalcia come to feed and grow fat.

These do not murmer immoderately at the pastures, but as the beasts are removed in detail the grass serves for grazing purposes even down to the ground. After the Revolution of September, which promised to correct all abuses and repair all matters of injustice, Lopez de Ayala, before known as a dramatic author, recruited in the lower part of the Spanish Parnassus an army of functionaries, magistrates and administrators unprovided for, with whom the employees then in Cuba were to be

superceded, who, at any rate, knew something of their duties.
" Good mana for these Gaditanos, said the Creoles, for us there
has been no change, except in masters." The thought which
gave voice to these words is that they wished the mana to fall
likewise into their own hands, and this is quite natural, inasmuch as they pay the expenses.

Ah ! the revolution of September is not destined, it seems to im-
prove matters more than the other *pronounciamientos* of a change
ministry, of constitutions, of former reigns.

Poor sheep how you are always sheared ! To this everything
comes as said Saco, renowned and respected Son of Cuba,
this money question is of more consequence than the political.
If Cuba were not, in fact, considered to be so rich, the question
economical would not be so deplorable. Spain must have her
hands free, which she can then, at pleasure, put into the money
bags of Cuba, and will never consent that this privilege shall be
taken away by the adoption of a *regime* colonial, founded upon
the principles of *autnomia* (free government, in all things, recog-
nizing only the sovereignty of Spain). This the Creoles well
understand,, and for this reason those who have taken up arms
will not be ready to lay them down.

From these resulted the scrupulous slowness of the money
dealers, who demanded of the Minister other guaranties or the
revision of the contract. The Minister thus replied : The Constitution of 1837 declares that the Ultramarine provinces shall
be governed by especial laws. But as these have not been promulgated, and until this is done, the Royal Power is fitted to govern them according to its will, to decree the imposts and employ them as to it shall seem fit without having to consult the
Cortes. For this reason the government of the Queen has the
perfect right, without the vote of the ,Cortes, to hypothecate the
income from its possessions beyond sea and contract the loan in
question. Is this not clear ? This was not sufficiently so for
the bankers, who prefered to lose the deposit made.*

If General Dulce on his arrival, clothed as he was with dis-
cretional powers, had proclaimed and organized such a regimen,

---

* This was paid by the provisions of a new loan of 100,000,000 francs celebrated with
the Provisional Government. The rate was 12½ per cent.

he would assuredly have given the death blow to the revolution, because all the moderate and sensible portion, of the population, which is the wealthiest and most influential, would have rallied around him. Either induced by persuasion or force, unfortunately, he did not comprehend the situation, or did not hold sufficient powers. He was impelled forward by a ridiculous pride of which the Spanish statistics have given so many proofs as well as by a desire to preserve the milk cow for all those called to govern her, or else Dulce or the government preferred to conquer the revolution by arms and punishments inflicted And we behold the spectacle of revolutionists shooting rebels for the same fault that they themselves have committed. The men most compromised in the last revolution are the Dulces, the Letonas, the Escalantes, the Caballero de Rodas, those who have solicited or accepted the *honor* of going to Cuba to represent such a roll, not to mention General Prim, the hero of the *pronunciamientos*, and of the last revolution, who has offered in full parliament to go with the whole Spanish army, if that were necessary. to avenge the honor of insulted Castile, and conserve the national integrity. But, I believe that the illustrious General, with his good Toledo blade, and the entire Spanish army would do better not to go to America. Waiting for this event, the Spanish people who pretend to give much attention to business, would do well not to occupy themselves with the just complaints of the Cubans and of the actual situation. It would seem that the matter was critical for all, and that the quickest solution would be better both for Spain and Cuba. The time has gone by when the lips of the Ever Faithful, the daughter of Spain, can be firmly sealed up, those lips on which if a generous voice had lifted itself in Parliament, or in the press, it would have encountered a minister to reply to the point in this manner : " Hear well, no murmur reaches us from the other side of the Atlantic, Cuba demands nothing, she asks for reforms of no kind, and if this were not so, who has hindered her for so many years from demanding them ?" A voice coming from exile answered : " How could she demand them with her press full of sarcasms, her corporations without enterprise, and her inhabitants deprived of the right of holding public meetings or of representation?" On the other hand—how many conspiracies, howm any insurrections has the government not been called upon to put down? How much blood has there been spilt in the struggle and on the scaffold? How many sons oi Cuba have been obliged to abandon their property, their families, their country, all that they loved to free themselves from persecutions? The list would be very large, likewise, it would be full of conspiracies, because in the last thirty years there have been more than sixteen. The silence is not because she has no aspirations, it is the silence of sarcasm. So it was decided to call representatives to Madrid, without other rights than to come to discuss, in the ante-chamber of the Ministry, plans of reform in company with an equal number of commissioners elected by the government, and known in advance to be enemies of every radical reform. They were invited by the minister to treat of all questions freely except three : political, religious, and monarchical unity, and were dismissed after having been humiliated and confounded, without other advantage than bringing along with them for their fellow citizens a summary of taxes larger than ever, in the preparation of which they hae not been permitted to participate.

The position we have painted is indeed gloomy, but in truth it is none other than the truth, to a certain extent, softened.

It will now be understood whether upon Cubans or Spaniards the responsibility shall rest for a separation, now almost realized, between the Mother Country and the Colony.